Andy Croft has written or edited over 80 books – poetry, fiction, biography and non-fiction. He has worked as a writer in residence in several prisons, including HMPs Holme House and South Yorkshire.

FORTY-SIX QUID
AND
A BAG OF DIRTY WASHING

FORTY-SIX QUID
AND
A BAG OF DIRTY
WASHING

ANDY CROFT

First published in Great Britain in 2014

Diffusion
an imprint of
SPCK
36 Causton Street
London SW1P 4ST
www.spckpublishing.co.uk

ISBN 978-1-908713-02-5

Typeset by Graphicraft Limited, Hong Kong
First printed in Great Britain by Ashford Colour Press
Subsequently digitally reprinted in Great Britain

Produced on paper from sustainable forests

For everyone with whom I had the privilege of working at HMP Moorland and HMP Lindholme, especially Jacquesy and Insy for their help and advice.

Contents

1

Freedom

———•◦•———

Barry was grinning like an idiot. Today was going to be brilliant. How could it not be? He was a free man. Free at last!

Anything could happen today. He could do anything he wanted. And whatever he did would be brilliant, because it would be his choice. He had been allowed so few choices for so long. And now he could choose anything on the menu. The right to make decisions felt like an under-used muscle. He needed to start exercising it. Bring it on!

He felt the warm sunshine on his face as he stared out of the window at the unfamiliar landscape of flat fields and straight roads. The bus was passing through small villages whose names he didn't know. It was funny to think that he had lived just down the road for so long. The people getting on and off the bus had been his neighbours. But he had never met them. They didn't know his name. And now he was suddenly leaving without saying goodbye.

The roads were busy. Barry had never seen so many SUVs before. People were going to work. Taking their kids to school. Going shopping. Running. Walking their dogs. All the ordinary things that other people did every day. As they passed a primary school he watched a man bend down to tie his son's shoelaces. The little boy looked up and waved at the bus. Barry started to wave back, then he stopped, embarrassed.

He suddenly felt like a stranger. All the years he had been in prison, these people had been getting on with their lives. Growing up, getting jobs, falling in love, having children, falling out of love. Meanwhile his life had been on hold. It was like someone had pressed the Pause button on the video of his life. And now they had suddenly pressed Play. Not for the first time in his life, Barry wished he could find the Rewind button.

A woman got on the bus and sat down opposite him. She was a bit old for Barry, but she had nice legs. He could smell her perfume. He tried to imagine her life. She wasn't wearing a wedding ring, but that didn't necessarily mean anything. Did she have children? Was she happy? Had someone told her they loved her this morning? He hoped so.

Barry smiled at the woman, but she looked away. He knew what she was thinking. It must be obvious. His clothes for one thing. The plastic bag of washing for another. And of course prison had its own special perfume. Chips, paint, floor polish and fags. The lad in the laundry had washed Barry's clothes last night, and this morning he had begged a bit of aftershave from Gaz. But he knew it would take a long time to wash the smell of prison out of his skin.

Right now the lads would be in the workshops. Mo would be doing his Toe-by-Toe in Education. Gaz would be sorting out the books that had come into the library last night. Mr Banks would be arguing with someone about last night's football. He grinned at the memory of the men with whom he had shared so much time.

It was strange to think that he wouldn't see them any more. It was even stranger to think that they were all still there, while he was out. Here he was on a bus, trying not to stare at the legs of the woman opposite, and they were still stuck inside the machine.

They said that a good prison worked like clockwork. But then prison was like a huge clock. Everyone inside was just a tooth on a cog on a wheel. Serving time. Doing time. Wasting time.

Most of the lads inside, Barry included, had wasted their time before they went to prison. And what was their punishment? To waste even more time. Watching daytime TV, staring out of the window, dreaming of fast cars, fast bucks and a quick leg-over. It didn't make any sense.

Barry had grown up on this last sentence. He was no longer the daft lad he used to be. He knew that. He had kept his head down, done his courses, stayed clean and kept out of trouble. He was ready to go back into society. Rehabilitated, they would call him. But this was nothing to do with the system. If he had changed, it was because of Gaz.

What do you think?

Why does Barry feel like a 'stranger'?

Why do you think Barry wishes he could press the Rewind button?

What do you think the woman on the bus thinks about Barry?

2

Gaz

———•◦•———

Barry had been padded up with Gaz when he moved onto Houseblock 5. They had hit it off from the start. Gaz was older than Barry, and he had seen a lot more of the world. He had also done a lot more time. He looked after Barry and took him under his wing. He was like the older brother Barry never had.

After a few weeks they offered Barry a single pad, but he had opted to stay with Gaz. By then they were mates. They had shared everything – biscuits, books and burn. They had shared stories about growing up, about the different jails they had been in, about girls they had known. Gaz had taught him how to play chess, introduced him to books and shown him what to read. He had taught him how to think for himself. The last two years they had worked together as library orderlies. They had shared their lives for the best part of four years.

But now Barry was a free man. He was free to do anything he wanted. For the first time in years, he didn't have to ask to go to the toilet. He could walk more than two hundred yards without having to wait for someone to open a door. He didn't have to eat with a plastic knife and fork any more. He could even watch an 18 DVD! All the simple pleasures of life were his again – a hot bath, a walk in the rain, a flutter on the horses, a pint, a curry. If he was lucky he might even end up sharing someone's bed before the end of the weekend.

Now he and Gaz belonged to different worlds. Different planets. Different time zones. This morning Barry had given Gaz the last of his burn and his copy of George Jackson's *Soledad Brother*. Gaz had put his arm round him and muttered something about meeting again 'on the other side'. But they both knew this wasn't going to happen for a long time. Gaz was IPP-ed, so the only place they were likely to meet again was inside. And Barry didn't want to go back there. Not ever. Not even to see Gaz.

It wasn't that jail was hard. Most lads soon got used to the loss of freedoms and the petty restrictions. Anyway, jail had its compensations –

good mates, strong friendships, time to think. But not many people found a way of dealing with the endless boredom, or with the inescapable sense of wasted time.

People called prison 'doing time'. But it was really the opposite – prison was about *undoing* time. In prison you undid time, day by day, hour by hour, picking at the stitches of your life until time began to unravel. There was no time in prison. Christmas, bank holidays and weekends all slipped past in a blur of boredom. There was no weather in prison either, no seasons, no sense of the year turning on its axis.

He breathed in deeply. No point thinking about all that now. There was no way he was going back. This time he knew he wasn't going to blow it. He had been looking forward to this day for such a long time. And now it had finally arrived. Unbelievable. He was a free man. All he owned in the world was his forty-six quid discharge grant and a bag of dirty washing. Freedom! The world really was his oyster. He could do anything, talk to anyone and go anywhere.

But first he had to see Abi.

What do you think?

Is Barry right to describe prison as a 'waste of time'?

What does the word 'freedom' mean to you?

What are you most looking forward to when you get out?

3

The other side of the glass

The bus pulled into the car park in front of the station. Barry's train wasn't due for another half-hour, so he walked round the square enjoying the weather, grinning like a meerkat in the bright sunshine.

The smell of baking from the bread shop on the corner reminded him that he was hungry. Barry couldn't remember the last time he had tasted a proper cheese pasty. In fact, he couldn't remember the last time he had eaten proper hot food. He joined the queue inside the shop. Then he saw the price.

He bought a packet of crisps instead and ate them on a bench outside the station. Then he bought some burn and some papers in the newsagent next door. They were even more expensive than the canteen. He rolled a tab and sparked up. On the other side of the square a traffic warden was checking parked cars. The woman from the bus came out of a flower shop.

Some office workers were eating their sandwiches by the fountain.

It was five past on the station clock. Barry showed his travel pass at the barrier. The ticket inspector looked at him. Maybe Barry was just imagining it, but he felt that the bloke was judging him. Well, he had done his time. He was a free man now.

On the train he made his way along the coaches until he found an empty seat by a window. The young Asian woman in the seat opposite was working on a laptop. So was the student next to her. Barry looked round. The whole carriage was full of people tapping away at keyboards or mobiles.

Once again he found himself wondering about the lives of his fellow travellers. That bloke in the yellow shirt – what did he do when he wasn't checking spreadsheets? Did he worry about his weight? The young Asian woman – was she in an arranged marriage? Was she a Muslim? Was she happy? What would any of them say if they knew that they were sharing the carriage with an ex-con?

Barry glanced at the books in front of the student. It looked like he was studying maths. Barry had been good at maths at school. In fact, it was the only thing he had been any good at. He had done Levels 1 and 2 maths on this last sentence. He had wanted to take A-level maths, but the education department had told him they didn't have anyone who could teach it. So he had worked as a cleaner on the wing instead. Typical joined-up prison thinking. But then Gaz had suggested he put in an app to work as a library orderly.

That job had helped the last two years pass. Barry had liked the librarians and had got on well enough with the library officer. He had loved the smell of all those books. Especially first thing in the morning. After the confinement of their pad on the 2s, the library always seemed light and airy. And apart from the chapel it was the only room in the jail with a carpet. Of course, there were always some lads who wanted him to nick DVDs or newspapers for them. But Gaz taught him how to say no. It was far too good a job to risk just to keep some idiot happy on the landing.

Barry looked out of the train window. Back gardens. Old men in their allotments. A child on a garden swing. He was amazed how ordinary everything seemed. Of course to everyone else it was just an ordinary day. They had no idea just how special today was for Barry.

At the same time, Barry wanted to be like them. He wanted to be ordinary. Like those scaffolders unloading their truck. Like that woman in shorts mowing her lawn, enjoying the sun. Or that postman weighed down by his bag. He had been cut off from all this for so long. Barry wanted to be part of it, to be the other side of the glass.

Soon they were passing through open countryside. A couple of horses in a field tried to race the train. A barge was waiting for some lock gates to open. They passed some kids playing football on a school field. Barry was glad he didn't have any children. At least none that he knew about. The other lads always said that children made a sentence go even slower. The only times he had ever seen tears inside were on the walkways coming back from a visit.

What do you think?

Do you think the ticket inspector was judging Barry, or is he being paranoid?

What do you think Barry means when he says he wants to be 'normal'?

Why do you think Barry is happy not to have any children?

4

Nan

———•◦•———

Barry had never had much of a family. His older sister was somewhere in New Zealand, his brother last heard of in London. They had both left home when he was small. Since his nan died last year, Abi was his only family. Barry was only three years older, but he had always thought of Abi as his baby sister.

He couldn't remember much about their mum. Just the smell of nail-varnish, rum and black, and menthol fags. She walked out one Christmas, soon after Abi was born. Just went off. Like a piece of old cheese, his nan used to say. Their dad had tried his best to bring them up. But he didn't have a clue really. Anyway, he was never at home. There was always someone who needed a motorbike fixing. The patch of grass behind their house had looked more like a scrapheap than a garden. When he wasn't mending bikes he was riding his own, a big old Harley that smelled of oil and burnt rubber.

After school Barry and Abi used to walk round to their nan's for their tea. She made them sit at the kitchen table instead of eating in front of the TV. She used to cook proper old-fashioned meals for them. Liver and onions and mashed potatoes. Lamb chops. Shepherd's pie. Rhubarb crumble and custard. And always fish and chips from round the corner on a Friday.

Nan had a real fire too. The rest of the house was freezing, but the front room was always baking. When she was in a good mood they used to play cards after tea in front of the fire, on an old green-baize table. Mostly kids' games like King in the Corner and rummy. If she was in a really good mood, she used to bring out a tin of treacle toffee. Home-made, of course. Sometimes they used to stay over. Other times their dad would collect them on his way back from the lock-up garage where he worked. If Barry possessed any happy memories, it was of this part of his childhood. Just Nan and Abi and him, warm and safe.

After their dad's accident, Social Services had wanted to put them into care, but Nan had taken them in. It must have been hard for her. It wasn't her fault that he had gone off the rails. She was far too old to be looking after two kids. But by then Barry was running rings round her. Soon after he moved to the comp, he began nicking off school and getting into trouble. It must have been around then that he first met Little Chris and the lads.

It must have done her head in, but his nan never gave up on him. The only time she had said anything was the first time he was excluded from school. She had really lost her temper then. But whatever she had tried to tell him, he wasn't listening. Barry didn't like to think of the number of times his nan had collected him from the police station. She was just starting on the chemo when he started his last sentence. He remembered her face in court, grey and sad and scared-looking. Of course they wouldn't let him out for her funeral. Not even in cuffs.

'Excuse me – are you all right?' It was the Asian woman opposite. Barry stared at her. Then he realized that there were tears running down his cheeks. He wiped his face on the back of his sleeve.

'No,' he stammered. 'I mean yes. Yes, I'm all right.' The other passengers were staring at him.

'Are you sure?' asked the woman.

'I'm fine,' he smiled. 'I'm fine. I'm just happy. Really.'

The woman didn't look like she believed him.

'No, but thanks. I'm fine.' The train was slowing down. This was Barry's stop.

'Honest. No worries. I'm just a bit emotional,' he said, standing up and getting down his bag from the rack. 'You see, it's just that today, today is . . .'

The woman looked at him, expectantly.

Barry grinned. 'Today's my birthday.'

What do you think?

Why do you think Barry went 'off the rails' when he was at school?

What are your happiest childhood memories?

Why do you think Barry is crying on the train?

5

The invisible man

———•◆•———

The sun was still shining as Barry walked down
the hill from the station into town. In the
distance he could see the floodlights of the
football stadium. This was his town, his home.
It was where he belonged. Over there was the
skateboard park where he had broken his wrist
trying to railside down the steps. On the left
was the Grand Hotel, famous for the fights at
chucking-out time.

Barry had walked these streets a thousand
times. He had walked them in prison dreams.
He sometimes felt he could find his way around
the town with his eyes shut. Like the statue of
blindfolded justice still standing outside the
County Court.

But he could also see how much had changed.
The Town Hall clock tower was cleaner than
he remembered. The Odeon was now a carpet
shop. The huge TV screen outside the library
was definitely new. There was a kebab takeaway

where a video shop used to be. Running along the edge of the pavement was a line of new blue bollards. The Queen's Head was now boarded up and derelict. It was as if someone had moved the pieces in the middle of a game of chess. Everything was the same and yet somehow changed. Or was it the other way round? Nothing, someone once said, is constant but change.

Barry rolled a tab and sparked up. This was going to take some getting used to. It wasn't just the buildings that had changed. The people were somehow different too. So far he hadn't seen a single face he recognized. Perhaps they had replaced all the people with aliens. Or maybe he was the alien. These people were all so busy with their lives. Barry seemed to be the only person enjoying the weather. He may have missed the town but he wasn't sure the town had missed him. No one in the crowds pushing their way in and out of the shopping centre seemed to even notice him. It was like he was in a zombie movie. Perhaps if they did notice him they would tear him to pieces.

Of course no one knew he was getting out today. So it wasn't that Barry had expected a brass band to meet him at the station, or big yellow ribbons hanging from every tree. But he had the feeling that the town had forgotten him. He felt as if he was invisible.

He stopped in front of a discount shoe shop and checked his reflection. Well, at least he hadn't turned into a vampire. He stared at himself in the glass. You talkin' to me? You talkin' to me? You talkin' to me? Then who the hell else are you talkin' to . . . you talkin' to me? Well, I'm the only one here . . .

He was going to end up looking like Travis Bickle if he wasn't careful. He could do with a bit of a make-over. For one thing, he badly needed a new shirt. And a new pair of trainers. The tracksuit trousers he had on were looking old before he went to prison. And he definitely needed a mobile.

But all that was going to cost a lot more than forty-six quid (less the cost of a packet of crisps, some papers and tobacco). Maybe one of the lads would be able to sell him a mobile. On tick, of course. With a bit of luck they would be in the Coach and Horses later. Maybe one of the lads would sub him some money.

The problem was that most of his best mates weren't around any more. Tommo and Fish were still inside. Rich was supposed to be working somewhere in Scotland, although no one had heard from him for ages. Mickey G and Mel were running her dad's bar in Salou. No one knew where Belly was. Dean was dead. And already memories of Gaz seemed to reach him like light from a distant star, from a long time ago, in a galaxy far, far away . . .

What do you think?

Why does Barry feel invisible?

Has the town changed? Or has Barry?

Why does Barry think he looks like Travis Bickle?

6

Lucky

'Got a light, mate?'

The Asian bloke was standing outside the betting shop on the corner, struggling with a lighter. He looked stressed.

'Sure.' Barry gave him his matches. 'This place new? I don't remember it being here. Didn't it used to be a video shop?'

'Depends what you mean by new. They're all over town now. It's them slot machines.'

'Slot machines?' Barry rolled a tab and sparked up. 'You mean they've got slot machines in there?'

'Fixed-odds betting machines. Where've you been, mate? Dead simple. Just like playing the arcades. You could be a millionaire!'

Barry had to admit that this bloke didn't look much like a millionaire. But he had heard plenty of stories about lads getting out and winning a small fortune on a quick bet. They were probably invented. The kind of hopeless fairy tale that lads in prison like to tell each other. But then again, it was always mathematically possible. And a quick win would certainly solve all his problems.

Inside there were four machines on the far wall. They were all busy. He looked at the TV screen. There was a race from Doncaster in five minutes. He looked down the list of runners. He didn't know the names of any of the horses, but one of them was called Dirty Washing. It was running at twenty to one. Maybe it was a good omen. Favourites don't always win, he told himself.

Some people spent their lives following horse racing, studying form and developing complicated systems. Barry preferred to take a punt on a horse's name. He didn't need to know anything about the horse, the stable or the rider. If he liked the name of the horse, he would put his shirt on it. Gaz once said that this explained why he had such a good tan.

Barry picked up a slip off the counter. As usual, most of the biros were broken. Eventually he found one that worked. How could he resist a horse with a name like this today? Ten quid each way could earn him two hundred and fifty. He could buy a mobile, shirt, jeans and trainers and still have some change. Or he could use it as a deposit on somewhere to live. He imagined Abi's reaction when he showed her round the flat.

The Asian bloke saw what Barry was doing. 'You're joking, aren't you? Waste of time and money, mate. Listen, you want to put your money on Take My Advice.'

But Barry wasn't listening. The spell was broken. He shook his head. Only a complete idiot would risk all his money on a horse. He went outside, rolled another tab and sparked up. That was a close shave. How could he have even considered it? He tried to imagine what Gaz would have said.

On the TV inside the shop, the race commentator was working himself into the usual fever. Barry needed to watch himself. He felt the money in his pocket, just to make sure that it was safe. But safe from what? Safe from his own stupidity. He thought of something Gaz had said a couple of nights ago. What's the difference between a wise man and an idiot? Answer: forty-six quid and a bag of dirty washing.

The Asian bloke came out for another fag. He looked even more stressed than before.

'Well?' asked Barry.

'Well what?'

'Doncaster.'

'What about it?'

'Who won?'

'Who won? You did, you lucky bastard!'

What do you think?

Why do you think Barry decided not to put his money on the horse?

What do you think Gaz's advice would have been?

What would you have done?

7

Big Brother

The bail hostel on Park Road was a big old house. Barry had stayed here once before. It must have been a nice place to live when it was first built. But now it had a sad look, like a woman who can't admit she has lost her youth. Or like a birthday cake left out in the rain.

Someone had tried to tart up the place by painting the brickwork bright yellow. Perhaps it had looked good on the colour chart, but it made the place look cheap and somehow insincere. The downstairs windows were barred. The front garden was now a staff car park, watched over by the unsleeping eyes of CCTV cameras. Welcome to the Big Brother House, thought Barry. 'Abandon hope, all ye who enter here.' He pressed the buzzer on the intercom and waited.

Barry hated bail hostels. These days they were known as 'approved premises'. But they were still the worst place to put someone straight out of jail. In some ways they were worse than prison. You had to put up with all the usual petty restrictions of the place at the same time as you were expected to handle your new-found freedom. He knew lads who had come back from bail hostels after only a couple of weeks. They couldn't cope with the pressure. Half the time the staff behaved as though you were all serial killers. The rest of the time they treated you like naughty children. Anyway, it didn't take much to be recalled – a missed appointment, a misunderstanding, an argument. There was always at least one member of staff who couldn't wait to send you back.

The door was opened by a blousy woman in her forties, big hair and dangly earrings.

'You must be . . .'

'Barry,' he held out his hand. 'I think you're expecting me.'

'I'm just putting the kettle on. How do you like it?'

She disappeared into the kitchen before Barry could reply. He sat down on one of the orange bottom-of-the-range chairs in the foyer. There was a poster on the wall. 'No alcohol. No smoking. No non-prescription drugs.'

She came back with two mugs of tea. 'I'm Barbara, and I am your key-worker. While you are with us I will help you formulate an action plan to ensure compliance, rehabilitation and the management of risk, to set appropriate objectives, review progress and refer you to specialist agencies when relevant.'

The tea was so sweet it was undrinkable. In prison Barry had given up drinking tea with sugar. But this was sugar with tea. Does he take sugar? No, he doesn't! But he decided not to say anything. He didn't want to get off on the wrong foot with this woman. He tried to swallow the stuff without gagging.

She gave Barry a booklet listing the hostel's rules, punishments and rewards. 'As part of the core regime residents are expected to participate in daily resident meetings and interventions such as tenancy awareness, independent living and accredited training for numeracy and literacy.'

When she had finished her tea she showed Barry round the place. Kitchen. Pool room. TV room. Dining room. There was no sign of any other residents. The walls were painted in the usual cheerful Home Office mustard green. The carpets looked like they could do with a good hoover. There were CCTV cameras everywhere. Barry had read somewhere that there were now over six million CCTV cameras in the UK. Half of them seemed to be in this hostel.

Barry's room was on the top floor, under the eaves. The walls, of course, were mustard green. The single bed looked like it had seen better days. There were cigarette burns on the windowsill, right beneath the No Smoking sign.

She gave Barry a towel. At least it wasn't mustard green. 'All residents must pay towards the cost of living in a hostel, including bed linen and towels. If you are on benefits then part or all of your rent may be paid direct to the hostel. You will be expected to be out of bed by eight forty-five in the morning and available to take part in purposeful activities as agreed with your Offender Manager and the hostel staff. You will be required to account for your movements when you are not in the hostel. Curfew is from eleven p.m. to six a.m.'

She went downstairs to the office to complete the paperwork while Barry unpacked. As he looked round the room he felt a sudden longing for the pad he had shared with Gaz. Compared to this room, it had seemed like a home, with his football posters on the wall and Gaz's books on the windowsill.

He looked out of the window. Behind the hostel was a cemetery. He watched a young couple pushing a buggy on the paths between the headstones. Two women were jogging. Some teenagers were trying to play with a frisbee. Not for the first time, Barry had the feeling that life was happening to other people, but not to him.

He wanted to be down there with these people, instead of up in the clouds, behind the glass. It was time for his new life to begin.

What do you think?

What does Barry mean when he describes bail hostels as being 'worse than prison'?

Why do you think that Barbara puts sugar in Barry's tea?

What's wrong with mustard green walls?

8

Little Chris

───────

Two hours later Barry emerged from the hostel, dazed with all the instructions he was supposed to remember. Do this, don't do that. Remember this, forget that. It was like being back in primary school. Infantilization, that's what Gaz called it. The system keeps telling you to act like a grown-up, but it insists on talking to you as if you were a kid.

'Oi, Baz!'

Only one person ever called him that. Anyway, Barry would know that husky voice anywhere. It was like something out of a low-budget horror film. Little Chris.

No one could remember why or how Little Chris got his name. Unless it was supposed to be a joke. At school he had been a fat bully. If you were his mate he could be funny, but he was a nightmare if he didn't like you. Barry remembered the way Little Chris used to tax packets of crisps off smaller kids. Then there was that Polish boy. For some reason, Little Chris had decided the kid was gay, and that it was his job to make his life hell. It had been funny for a while, but Little Chris never knew when to stop. And by then none of them knew how to stop him.

'All right, mate.'

Little Chris was leaning out of the window of a blacked-out SUV. He was wearing a pair of shades. He looked exactly like a drug-dealer straight from a TV soap.

'Been a while, Baz. Do you want a lift?'

Barry and Little Chris had both gone to the same schools, the same PRUs and the same YOIs. They were smoking weed by the time they were fourteen. At fifteen they were drinking in the same pubs. They were twocking cars at sixteen. By the time they were eighteen they were out grafting. And on the gear.

Someone inside had told Barry that Little Chris had cleaned up and had now set himself up as a bit of a player. He was no longer a small-time dealer, but higher up the food chain. Judging by the car, he was doing all right for himself.

'No, mate. I'm enjoying the walk. It's been a long time . . .'

'When did you get out?'

'Today.'

'You're joking? Today? Baz, my old friend, this calls for a celebration. What you doing tonight? You want to come to a party?'

The last thing Barry wanted was to spend his first night with Little Chris. He knew what his parties were like. 'Dunno, no plans yet. Coach and Horses, I suppose.'

'See you there, then. And remember, the drinks are on me tonight. And the girls,' he winked.

'OK,' said Barry, starting to walk away, 'maybe see you later.'

But Chris didn't seem to be in a hurry to go.

'Do you need anything, Baz?'

'Like what?'

'You know what I mean. First weekend out, you want some subby. You want a toot. Maybe you fancy a dig after all this time. But you need to be careful. Take it slowly. You need to know where it's been.'

'No, mate. Thanks but I'm clean as a whistle.'

'Is that right, Baz?'

'That's right, Chris.'

Chris took off his shades and stared at him.
'You looking for work, Baz?'

'Yeah. I mean no.'

'Got something lined up?'

'No. I mean yeah.'

'You have or you haven't. Which is it, Baz?'

Barry knew what Chris was going to say next.

'It's just that I was wondering when you are
going to start paying me back.'

'No worries, Chris. You will get your money.'
Barry was aware that he sounded nervous.
Perhaps he was. 'Honest. I just need some time
to get things sorted.'

'How much was it, Baz? Remind me. How much
of my money did you lose?'

'How much?'

'Yes, how much? How much do you owe me?'

'Eight hundred quid.'

'That's a lot of money, Baz. I need to know
when you are going to start paying me back.
I've been waiting a long time already.'

'Just give me a few weeks, Chris. I'll pay you.'

'Things are changing round here, Baz. My business
is expanding fast. I could do with a bit of help.'

Barry could imagine what kind of help he had in mind. But he wasn't interested. The problem was that you couldn't easily refuse Chris. He owed him the money. And Chris never took maybe for an answer.

'Bit of this, bit of that. Driving mostly. You still got your licence? You might even get to travel abroad. See the world! Time you got yourself a passport. Ever been to Amsterdam, Baz?'

What do you think?

Why doesn't Barry want to go to one of Little Chris's parties?

What kind of job do you think Little Chris wants Barry to do?

Is working for Little Chris better than no job at all?

9

Thinking

In the Coach and Horses Barry ordered a pint and a packet of peanuts and sat down at a table in the corner. It would be cheaper to buy some cans from a supermarket. But he couldn't take them back to the hostel. And he didn't fancy spending his first night drinking alone on a park bench.

Anyway, he needed to see Abi. He wanted to explain about his plan to get a flat for them both. The problem was that he didn't know where she was living. He hadn't heard from her since their nan died. He was hoping that there would be someone in tonight who might know her address.

It was a while since he had been in the Coach. Or in any pub for that matter. The barmaid was new. So was the karaoke machine. He stared at the pint on the table in front of him and licked his lips. He wanted to savour this moment. It was his first taste of alcohol since that lethal hooch on Houseblock 2. But the conversation with Little Chris kept going round and round inside his head.

Where was he going to find eight hundred quid? All he had in the world was forty-six quid and a bag of dirty washing. And that was disappearing fast. He felt the money in his trakkie bottoms. It was still there, but at two pound forty a pint it wasn't going to last very long.

Barry hadn't thought much about Little Chris or about the money while he was inside. For most people, a jail sentence meant a cancelling of debts. You went in owing someone and you came out with a clean slate. All square. But Chris didn't work like that. He was different. Ever since they were at school he had insisted on an eye for an eye and a tooth for a tooth. He didn't make threats. He just made demands.

The stupid thing was that Barry didn't really owe him any money at all. A few years ago Chris had asked him to deliver some phet to an address on the Meadows estate. He had got lost in the dark and stopped at an off-licence for directions. When he came out someone had nicked the car. And Chris had blamed him.

Barry needed to think. He went outside and sparked up. He didn't know what to think. Gaz had tried to teach him how to think. He used to make him stare out of the window for five minutes without speaking. Then he would ask him what he had been thinking about. At first Barry never knew how to answer, but eventually he learned how to think about what he was thinking. Gaz used to say that there was no point thinking something unless you knew why you thought it. Most people, he said, don't know what they think, never mind why they think it.

Gaz had slowly introduced him to bits of philosophy. Not fancy philosophy, but the real hard stuff – George Jackson, Huey Newton, Angela Davies, Chomsky, Fanon, Malcolm X. It had been an education all right. A kind of crash course in reading and thinking about the world. It had been his university. Barry hadn't always understood what he was reading. But he had enjoyed trying to get his head round this kind of stuff.

Last year he had submitted an essay about 'Rehabilitation' to the Koestler Awards. Highly Commended, they said. *Inside Time* even published one of his letters about the effects of government cuts on the library service in prisons. It was the 'Star Letter of the Month'. One of the librarians had cut it out and stuck it on the library noticeboard.

Barry finished his tab and went back inside. He wondered what Gaz was doing now. He could do with talking to him. Not that Gaz ever told him what to do. But he could help him think round a problem. And between losing Chris and finding Abi, Barry definitely had a problem.

What do you think?

What do you think Barry should do about the eight hundred quid he owes Chris?

What kind of books has Barry been reading?

What advice do you think Gaz would give Barry?

10

Friday night

'Barry, mate! Welcome back to the land of the living!' The Coach and Horses was rammed and incredibly loud. Everyone seemed to be shouting. Barry didn't remember pubs being this noisy. Maybe he had forgotten. But he wished someone would turn down the volume switch.

'What you drinking?'

Barry lifted his pint to indicate that he already had one.

'No, mate, I insist. You must be parched.' The man turned to the girl behind the bar. 'Another pint for my friend when he's ready . . .'

As soon as Barry finished one pint, another appeared in front of him. Everyone in the pub seemed to want to buy him a drink. He didn't even know most of them. Billy and Tankz were there. Craig Daniels had called in earlier. Davy Dee was there with his new girlfriend. Plus some lads he vaguely knew from the Blackhall estate.

But that was it. If Barry was honest, these people were not really his mates.

Barry was trying his best to enjoy himself. This was supposed to be his party, after all. Everyone wanted to shake his hand and make jokes about the state of his arse. The weird thing was that everyone seemed to be talking at him. No one seemed to be talking *to* him. It was good to be here, but a bit distant, *muffled*. Like sex when you wear a condom.

There was a group of shrieking girls celebrating something on the next table. They were wearing bright pink tutus. It was either a hen night or some kind of student game. Whatever it was, they seemed to be enjoying themselves. Barry caught the eye of a girl with red hair; she smiled at him.

Perhaps it was the effect of too much beer on an empty stomach, but his hearing was becoming blurred. He had the strange feeling that people were talking about him as though he wasn't there. He felt like a ghost at his own funeral. This wasn't quite how he had imagined his first night of freedom.

Some people seemed to think he was a hero, just because he had been inside. As though it was a badge of honour. Proof that he was a real man.

He wanted to tell them that there is nothing glamorous about jail. That he was ashamed to have wasted so much time in prison. But the thought of prison made him think of Gaz. He felt suddenly homesick for the quiet pad they had shared.

On the other hand, everyone was trying hard to make him feel welcome. What was wrong with him? He needed to relax. He always knew it was going to be hard. Not quite as hard as it was for the old feller at the end of *Shawshank*, maybe. But suddenly living among so many people was going to take some getting used to.

Meanwhile, the pints were still arriving but Barry had stopped drinking. He couldn't possibly keep up. The room was beginning to tilt a bit at the edges. Time was going faster. But inside his head it was moving slowly. He felt like a footballer trying to get back into the rhythm of the game after being out for a long time with an injury. The ball kept flashing past, just out of reach. His mind was swimming round and round, like a lonely goldfish in a bowl. Perhaps Barry was the lonely goldfish. And just at this moment he wanted to hide among the weeds at the bottom of the tank.

He needed some fresh air. Outside in the pub car park he rolled a tab. The night was warm.

Despite the orange junk-light of the town, he could make out several constellations of stars. Gaz had taught him how to do this through the narrow barred window of their pad. Barry shook his head. It was strange to think that he was free while Gaz was still banged up. Even stranger to think that Gaz was maybe looking up at the same stars tonight.

What do you think?

Why isn't Barry enjoying himself?

Why do you think the people in the pub treat Barry as a hero?

How would you like to spend your first night of freedom?

11

Lisa

———— •◆• ————

'Can I join you?' Barry turned. It was the redhead. He nodded.

'God, it's so warm out here,' she said, lighting up. 'I love these summer nights, don't you?'

'I'm not John Travolta, you know.'

She smiled. 'You looked a bit lost in there. Are you OK?'

'It's weird,' said Barry. 'I have been looking forward to this for so long. And now . . .'

'And now what?'

'I dunno. I just don't seem to be able to relax, to enjoy myself. I think there must be something wrong with me.'

She took a swig from a bottle. 'How come you know Billy and Tankz? I haven't seen you around before.'

'I've been away. I mean, I've been – I've been away.'

The girl leaned towards him. 'But now you're home.'

He tried not to look at her cleavage. 'But that's just it. Doesn't feel like home any more.'

Barry didn't know why he was talking to this girl like this. He didn't even know her name. Maybe it was the beer. Maybe he just needed a stranger to talk at. Someone who didn't know him. She seemed sympathetic.

'The thing is – I've just got out from prison. This morning.' He waited for her to pull away, but she didn't. 'I can't explain, but it feels all wrong somehow. It's as though I don't belong here. I feel like I shouldn't be here.'

She put her hand on his arm.

'You know that Tom Hanks film, where he gets shipwrecked?'

'*Castaway*?'

'Yeah. You know how at the end he goes to this big party and there are all these people and all this food and he walks away? Well, at the moment I feel like walking away.'

'What's stopping you?'

'This is my home. Except that so far it doesn't feel like that. I feel like a ghost who has come

back to haunt the house where I used to live.
I can see and hear everything around me, but
no one can see me. I'm not really here. It's like
I'm in a dream. Or I'm watching myself in a film.'

'Not a John Travolta film, I hope.'

'A zombie film more like.' They both laughed.

'I'm Lisa, by the way.'

'Barry. Pleased to meet you, Lisa.' They shook
hands formally and laughed.

'I'm going back inside,' she said, finishing her
cig. 'Come and join us, if you like.'

'Thanks, I will,' he said, rolling another tab.
'I'll just finish this first.'

Barry watched Lisa walk across the car park. He
couldn't help noticing her long legs, the way she
swung her hips as she walked. She turned to wave
as she reached the door. He waved back. He liked
this girl.

He finished his tab and went back inside. The
pub was even noisier than before. In the lounge it
was standing room only. There was a darts match
in the back bar. And a big crowd in the pool
room. He could see Billy and Tankz on the fruit
machines by the toilets. The hen-party girls were
singing round the karaoke machine. But there
was no sign of Lisa.

There was a sudden roar of laughter from a group of lads by the bar. Barry looked across the room. The loudest laughter was from Little Chris. Still wearing shades. In the middle of the group, a girl was performing a joke lap dance, exaggerating her movements for laughs. She was wearing a boob tube, a short skirt and not much else. Barry thought she looked familiar, but her long hair was all over her face. It looked like she was really out of it. Every time she fell over, one of the lads caught her while the rest cheered. There were hands all over her, grabbing and squeezing her flesh, pulling up her top. She was so wasted she didn't seem to mind. Barry felt embarrassed for the girl. But mostly angry with the animals who were groping her.

Then he realized who it was.

What do you think?

Why does Barry compare himself to the Tom Hanks character in *Castaway*?

Why do you think Barry liked Lisa?

Who do you think the 'lap-dancing' girl is?

Why do you think Barry was angry at the 'animals' who were groping the girl dancing on the table?

12

Saturday morning

———◆•◆•◆———

Strange bed. Headache. Dry mouth. Barry slowly opened his eyes. Bright sunlight. Mustard-coloured curtains. He remembered where he was. Then he remembered who he was. And why his head was hurting. It was Saturday morning and he was back in the hostel with a hangover and a head full of trouble.

He had no idea how he had got back to the hostel. Tankz and Billy must have brought him back. He had no memory of getting into a taxi. Or getting out of one. As far as he knew, he had only drunk five pints, so his head shouldn't be hurting. But it was. Perhaps his system had forgotten how to cope with alcohol.

Then he remembered – Abi! What did she think she was doing? He thought again of those men laughing at her as they pawed and clawed at her body. The last thing he remembered was trying to speak to her before someone pulled him away. The memory of his kid sister flaunting herself like that in front of all those men made him feel sick. Why was she hanging around with Little Chris? Didn't she know what he was like? Barry had to find Abi and talk to her, to warn her about him.

He suddenly remembered Lisa. He thought about her legs. How she had listened to him moaning on. She must have thought he was mad, but she had let him talk. He had forgotten what it was like to talk to a woman. They were different. Not just in the obvious ways. Sometimes women were so different it was hard to understand them. But they were also different in good ways.

Of course she was attractive. But it had been good to be able to talk to her like that. Somehow he knew that she would understand. She hadn't judged him because of who he used to be.

He needed to talk to her again. There were so many things he hadn't told her. He wanted to talk to her about Abi. But he realized that he didn't know her address or her telephone number. He didn't even know her surname.

He stared at the ceiling. It was Saturday. Like bank holidays and Christmas, weekends were often the worst days in prison. While normal people felt a sense of freedom on a Saturday morning, in prison it usually meant bang-up for most of the day. Today was his first Saturday morning of freedom. He was a free man. He didn't have to go and collect his breakfast from the servery. He didn't have to put his name down for a shower, or wait at his door for gym to be called. He could do anything he wanted.

He crawled out of bed and into the shower. There was no shampoo, so he had to wash his hair with soap. He made a mental note to add a razor, shaving gel, toothpaste and a toothbrush to the list of things he needed to buy. It was strange to think that he no longer had to wait all week for canteen. He could walk into a chemist and buy whatever he wanted. Incredible.

Barry knew he ought to be feeling like a small kid waking up on Christmas morning. Instead he felt rubbish. He should have been more careful last night. It wasn't just the hangover. Everything had gone wrong. He felt as though he had let someone down. But who?

What do you think?

What does Barry mean when he says that women are 'different'?

How would you like to spend your first Saturday morning when you get out?

Who do you think Barry has let down?

13

Available for work

———————

It was going to be a scorcher. The shops were already busy by the time Barry had walked into town. He was peckish, but he only had just over thirty quid left. He would have to make do with another packet of crisps for breakfast. He caught sight of his reflection in a barber's window. Travis Bickle was still here. A decent haircut would have to wait until he had found a job.

After an hour walking round the town centre Barry realized that finding a job was not going to be as easy as it used to be. He asked at a newsagent, a paint shop, a garage, two supermarkets, a multi-storey car park, a pizza takeaway and a discount carpet shop. No one had any vacancies. And no one had any plans to take on anyone in the immediate future.

He was probably still banned from half the pubs in the town, but no one knew him in the King's Head, so it was worth a try. He took a deep breath and put on his brightest smile.

Inside a grey-looking old woman was wiping the tables.

'Be with you in a minute,' she wheezed.

'I don't want a drink. I'm looking for a job.'

'What job?'

'You tell me, love. The job you're going to give me.'

'Am I?'

'Well, are you in charge?'

'No. You need to talk to Mr Allsop, the manager.'

'Where can I find him?'

She disappeared out the back. Barry looked round the pub. This must have been a classy place once. High ceilings, cornices and leaded lights. Take out the fruit machines and the wide-screen TVs and it would soon look all right. He could picture himself cashing up at the end of the night and having a quiet, cosy drink . . .

'You got any experience of bars, young man?'

Barry guessed that this was Mr Allsop. The colour of his face suggested that he had been doing his bit to keep the brewery in profit.

'Well,' grinned Barry, 'I've certainly spent a lot of time drinking in them.'

'Sense of humour, I see.' It was obvious that Mr Allsop didn't have one.

'Customers like a bit of a laugh, I reckon.'

'As it happens, I could do with another pair of hands round here just now.' He looked Barry up and down as though he was a horse he was about to buy. 'Do you have any references?'

'No, but I'm a good worker. I won't let you down, Mr Allsop.'

'Previous employer?'

Barry hesitated. There was no point lying. Best to make a clean breast of it. 'I've been – I've been away. I mean – I've been. Look, I'll be honest with you, Mr Allsop. I've been inside. In prison. I've just got out. And I really want to find a job. Just give me a chance.'

Mr Allsop glared at Barry and folded his arms. 'You must think I'm stupid, son. I've got enough problems with smackheads and thieves in this place without putting one on the payroll. There's plenty of honest folk can't find work in this town at the moment. So you and your sort can get to the back of the queue. Go on, I mean it. Get out of my pub! Clear off!'

During the next couple of hours Barry tried a florist, a chip shop, a mini-supermarket, a bike shop and a greengrocer's. None of them had any vacancies. Or if they did, they clearly weren't going to give someone like Barry a chance. He was beginning to feel that he had the words 'EX-CON' tattooed on his forehead. Or was he becoming paranoid? How could he get a flat if he couldn't find a job? It could be ages before he received any benefit. And when he did they would deduct half of it to pay for the hostel. But what was he supposed to do till then?

Barry was just about to give up when he saw a sign in a newsagent's window: 'Paper Boy Wanted.' Barry went in.

'I've come about the job.'

The Asian woman behind the counter looked at him blankly over her glasses.

'What job?'

'Paper boy.'

The woman looked at Barry as though he was winding her up. 'You're not exactly a boy, are you?'

'I'm not made of paper either, but I could do the job. I used to have a paper round when I was younger.'

The woman sighed, as if she thought she was talking to someone with special needs.

'Look, I'm sorry, but we are really looking for someone younger for this position.'

'You mean you're discriminating against me just because of my age?'

'Yes, I mean no. I mean . . .'

'So why can't I apply for the job, then?'

The woman thought for a second. 'Have you got a bike?'

Austerity Britain was not the time or place to be looking for work. Barry knew that things were tough, but this was ridiculous. In the past he had always been able to find some kind of job. Most of them were rubbish jobs, badly paid and short-term. Not much Health and Safety. But even a rubbish job was better than no job.

The Job Centre was just across the road. But even that had changed. It was now called 'Jobcentre Plus'. 'Plus what?' thought Barry. Plus a locked door. Plus a notice saying that it was open from nine a.m. to five p.m. Monday to Friday. The place was shut. Perfect. Just what Barry needed to help him find a job.

What do you think?

Why should Mr Allsop give Barry a chance?

Why is a rubbish job better than no job at all?

What are your plans for finding a job when
  you get out?

14

The Big Issue

There was a *Big Issue* seller outside the Job Centre. 'All right, Barry?'

Barry thought he looked familiar.

'It's Barry, isn't it? Course it is. Houseblock 1. You were on the Threes. Derek. Derek Goodman. The table-tennis king?' He mimed a table-tennis slam. Barry remembered. The man had lost a lot of weight since he had seen him last. He looked rough.

'Derek! How you doing?'

'What does it look like?' he replied. 'I'm fifty-two, I'm homeless, I'm an ex-con with a bad habit and I'm selling *The Big Issue*. I'd say I'm doing rather well, wouldn't you?'

Barry remembered what Derek was like when he was on a roll.

'That Richard Branson, he wanted me to help him run his business empire, but I told him I was a bit busy right now.' He waved a copy of the magazine at Barry. '*Big Issue*, sir? Marketing and promotions, that's me. I'm a media tycoon these days, son.'

Barry grinned. 'How long you been doing this?'

'Since nine o'clock this morning. Seriously – six months. Not always here, though.' He nodded over his shoulder towards the door of the Jobcentre Plus. 'I'm not likely to sell many copies here during the week.'

Barry got out his burn. 'Do you want a smoke?'

'No thanks, son. They're bad for your health.' He looked round. Barry knew what was coming next. 'I don't suppose . . .'

'Sorry, mate,' said Barry. 'I'm clean. Honest.'

'Got any spare change? For old times' sake.'

'I would, but I'm skint. Completely flat stony broke.' Barry knew this sounded a bit lame. 'I only got out yesterday. And to be honest, I am struggling a bit. I've just spent all morning trying to find a job.'

Derek laughed, theatrically. 'A job? Not much chance of you finding a job round here, I'm afraid.'

'Why's that, then?'

'Don't they have newspapers in Her Majesty's hotels no more?'

'Not proper newspapers. Only *The Sun* and that.'

'Well, first off,' Derek began, 'there are two and a half million people in this country with no job. Second, towns like this still haven't recovered from the last recession. That old witch Thatcher did a lot of damage round here. Third, if there are any jobs, they are not going to start handing them out to the likes of you and me, are they? You stand more chance of getting a job inside than you do out here.'

'But –'

'Stands to reason, Barry. Look. What's the minimum wage? I'll tell you: six pound thirty-one an hour. How much do they pay you in prison? *Eighty pence a day.* So what does your average businessman do? He closes his factory, sacks all the workers and opens a prison workshop. Stands to reason, doesn't it? Jail provides a ready supply of cheap labour on the doorstep. You can't join a trade union in jail. And you certainly can't go on strike. Talk about slave labour. They won't even let you vote . . .'

'Yes, but –'

'They shut all the pits, the steel mills, the shipyards and the factories where our granddads and dads used to work. Meanwhile they're building more and more jails. It's not a coincidence, Barry. Think about it. The working population goes down and the prison population goes up. They're connected, see? Fewer real jobs means lower wages. Lower wages means more prisoners. And more prisoners means fewer jobs! Welcome to Coalition Britain!' He bowed like a magician who had just pulled a rabbit out of his sleeve.

'And that, ladies and gentlemen, is the end of the show.'

Derek moved through an imaginary audience pretending to take a collection in an imaginary hat. Barry left him counting the imaginary money. He needed to find Billy and Tankz. They might know where he could find Abi. With a bit of luck they would call in at the Coach and Horses on their way to this afternoon's game.

What do you think?

Why do you think Derek is so cynical?

To what extent is Derek right?

15

Guilty

He walked quickly across town, taking a short cut down a one-way street behind the shops. As he passed the line of cars parked on his right, Barry realized that he was checking the seats for bags. It was an automatic reflex. He stopped as soon as he realized what he was doing. He was still a bit of an idiot, but not a complete idiot.

Just then he passed a green Astra. On the front seat was a woman's coat. And sticking out from under the coat was a handbag. He could see a purse and a mobile. Easy. Barry looked round. The street was quiet. On the opposite side of the road an old lady was throwing bread to the birds. It would only take a few seconds. And it would solve his immediate problems. He imagined what Abi would say when he gave her the key to their flat. Of course, the phone probably wouldn't fetch much, but the bag looked quality. He looked down the street again. Then again at the bag. What could possibly go wrong? Everything. He grinned and started to walk away.

'Oi! What the hell do you think you're doing?'

Barry spun round. A tall woman in her early forties was running towards him.

'Me?'

'Yes, you. I saw you.'

'Saw me do what?'

'Get away from my car now.'

'Look, missus, I don't know what you're talking about. I haven't done anything, right?'

'Empty your pockets.'

'What?' This woman was mental. 'But I haven't done anything. Swear down.'

'Show me what's in your pockets.'

A large man in an overcoat came panting after her.

'What's going on, Susan?'

'I just caught this man breaking into the car.'

'No, you didn't!' Barry protested. 'Are you mad or just blind?'

'Look here, young man. Don't speak to my wife like that.'

'Tell him to empty his pockets, Brian!'

'Look, mate,' said Barry, 'this is doing my head in. I was *not* breaking into your car. Or anyone else's.'

'What were you doing, then?'

'Minding my own business.'

The man pulled out a mobile. 'I'm calling the police.'

Not a good idea. Barry knew what would happen if the police were called. The fact that he hadn't nicked anything was irrelevant. His record would speak for itself. He could imagine their faces as he walked back into Reception. He looked round. For a split second he thought about doing a runner, but that would only make things worse.

'I'm sorry, but I don't know what you're talking about.' Barry hoped they couldn't tell how desperate he was. 'Just because your wife's stupid enough to leave her bag on the front seat of your car, it doesn't mean that everyone who walks past is a thief, does it?'

The man peered doubtfully inside the car, then glared at his wife. 'Darling, how many times have I told you not to leave things in the car like this? It's an open invitation.'

'But he was going to break in, I know he was!'

He turned to Barry. 'It seems there's been some sort of mistake. I'm terribly sorry. Please accept this by way of an apology,' he said, reaching into the inside pocket of his waistcoat and offering Barry a crisp new tenner.

Barry stared at it. He didn't know what to say. Which was worse – being accused of something he hadn't done, or being paid off like this? He half expected the man to tell him to buy himself an ice cream. The man saw his hesitation and pulled out another ten-pound note.

'No hard feelings, son.'

Barry nodded and took the money. He wasn't in a position to refuse it. He smiled to himself. Twenty quid for *not* breaking into a car! Nice work if you can get it. He could make a living out of not breaking into cars. A bit like farmers being paid not to grow certain crops in their fields. The day was suddenly taking a turn for the better.

But as he walked away he knew there was part of him that was feeling guilty about something.

What do you think?

What might have happened if Barry had stolen the bag?

What do you think Barry is feeling when the man offers him the money?

16

Saturday night

By the time he had reached the Coach, Tankz and Billy had gone to the match. He watched a Premier League game on the pub's TV instead, carefully nursing a very slow pint through the afternoon. There was still no sign of them after the game. Maybe they had changed their post-match ritual. Barry walked back to the hostel for a kip.

By eight o'clock he was in the town centre again. He had to be in the hostel by eleven p.m. But three hours should be enough to find someone who knew where Abi lived. He looked in the Feathers, the Miners Arms and the Mucky Duck. He tried the new bars down by the marina. Still no luck. Then he remembered Billy saying something last night about Shakers, a new club that had just opened on Market Street. Barry wasn't in the mood to go clubbing. But he had to find out where Abi was living. He had to talk to her.

He found the club by the size of the queue outside. Ten minutes later he was inside. The noise hit him like a punch in the face. The place was heaving. Everything smelt of new paint, spilt drinks and sweat. He tried three different bars. He stood watching the dancers on the dance floor. It was Saturday night. Everyone was enjoying themselves, drinking, shouting and dancing. Everyone except Barry.

He was about to leave and go back to the hostel when he felt a tap on the shoulder. Lisa. She was wearing a green dress that set off her red hair beautifully. She was even prettier than he remembered. He felt ridiculously pleased to see her.

'Do you come here often?'

'What?'

'I said, do you come here often?'

'What?'

'I said – oh, never mind. Do you want a drink?'

'What?'

Barry took Lisa by the arm and steered her towards the bar. The music wasn't quite so loud there, but conversation was still impossible. Barry mimed lighting up and Lisa nodded.

They went outside for a smoke.

'You feeling better?' she asked.

'I'm feeling better for seeing you.'

'Aren't you a sweet-talking charmer?' she said, leaning forward to kiss him on the cheek.

She smelled lovely.

'No, I mean it,' said Barry. 'Nice dress.'

'Thanks.'

'Did you know that the Russian word for "fox" is Lisa?'

'You making this up?'

'No, it's true. I knew this Russian bloke inside once. Mad Vlad we called him. I don't know what his real name was. He told me some Russian words. Lisa the fox. Foxy Lisa. Goes well with your red hair.'

She laughed self-consciously and put her hand on his arm. 'Do you want to come to a party? At my house?'

'You own a house?'

'No, I rent a room in a house.'

'What kind of party?'

'A party. You know, where people enjoy themselves. Anyway, what's with all the questions? Do you want to come back to my place or not?'

Barry could guess what kind of party it would be. This was just the kind of situation he needed to avoid. Anyway, he had to be back at the hostel by eleven o'clock. But how could he explain all this to Lisa? And he didn't want to give her the wrong impression. He really liked this girl. He took a deep breath. Sod the hostel.

'Yeah, of course. I'd love to come.'

What do you think?

Why is Barry so pleased to see Lisa?

Which do you think is more important – being happy or being free?

If you were Barry, how would you decide whether to go to the party or back to the hostel?

17

Abi

————•◦•————

As Lisa paid for the taxi Barry recognized the noisy combination of loud music, shouted conversations and laughter coming from inside the terraced house. The place was packed.

He went into the kitchen to get drinks for him and Lisa. When he came out she had disappeared. The party had divided itself up along the usual lines – drinking in the kitchen, talking in the hall and dancing in the front room. In the back room the air was thick with the sweet smell of skunk. Someone standing in the doorway offered him a joint. Barry shook his head. He didn't want to fail a piss-test in the hostel just because of a stupid joint.

He went upstairs to look for Lisa. He had to climb over a girl sitting on the stairs texting. 'Excuse me, have you seen a girl with long red hair?'

The girl looked up from her mobile. It was Abi. She stared blankly at him.

'Abi, it's me, Barry!' He put down the cans he was holding.

She looked at him coldly. 'Who?'

'Barry! Who do you think?' He tried to put his arms round her shoulders. She flinched and pushed him away.

'What are you doing? It's me – I'm your brother, Abi!'

'That's funny. I don't have a brother. I used to have one, but he preferred spending time with his precious mates in jail to looking after me.'

'I'm not like that any more, Abi. I've changed. Honest.'

'Honest? That's an interesting word coming from you.'

Barry was frantic. 'Just listen to what I'm saying, will you?'

'No, you listen to me, Barry. How did Abi do in her GCSEs, Barry? Why did Abi get kicked out of college, Barry? You don't know, do you? You know nothing about me. You don't even know where I live. Where were you when Nan was poorly, Barry? I mean really poorly. Have you ever watched someone die, Barry? I know I have. And I had to do it all on my own. You were somewhere else, weren't you? Too busy "changing". I don't remember seeing you at the hospital when Nan went for her chemo, Barry. Or the radiotherapy. You weren't even at Nan's funeral, were you? Well, I was. So don't start trying to tell me that you've turned over a new leaf. Cos I'm not buying it.'

Barry didn't know what to say. 'Look, Abi, I'm sorry. I'm sorry. I'm sorry. I know I've been a rubbish brother. You don't have to tell me that. But I really am trying to change.'

'Oh yeah, you and Barack bleeding Obama! But is it change we can believe in, Barry?'

'Look at me. I'm clean. Proper clean this time. And, and – I'm trying to get a job. And when I get a job I can get a flat. Then we can move in together.'

'What?' She laughed. 'You're joking, aren't you? Live with you?'

'No, I'm not. I'm dead serious. Someone has to look after you. I don't like to see you hanging about with the wrong people.'

'Just piss off!' Abi shouted, pushing him. He grabbed the banisters to stop himself from falling. 'You can't just walk in here after all this time and tell me what to do. I'll see who I want, when I want. And I'll do what I want.'

'But Abi –'

Barry suddenly felt something cold against his cheek. He froze.

'What's going on?' said a familiar husky voice. 'Abi, are you all right? Is this toe-rag upsetting you?'

'Yeah, he is, Chris. He's upsetting me. Really upsetting me . . .'

What do you think?

To what extent do you think Abi is justified in being angry with her brother?

Why should she believe him when he says he has changed?

How can Barry convince her that he has changed?

18

Homesick

———•◦•———

Outside it was raining. It was a fine, warm summer rain. But Barry wasn't in the mood to enjoy it. This was *so* not what he wanted. He was walking the midnight streets, trying to sort his head out. It wasn't turning out to be the homecoming he had imagined. Or the big reunion with Abi he had been looking forward to for so long. Everything seemed impossible. Why was life so difficult? As far as he could see, life on the out consisted only of problems and temptations, frustrations and disappointments.

He tried to think. Somehow he had to get Abi away from Little Chris. But he also had to pay Little Chris what he owed him. If he accepted his offer of a job he would get his hands on some money. And he might be able to keep an eye on Abi. But if he worked for Chris, sooner or later he would end up back inside. No two ways about it. Then he wouldn't be able to look after her at all. But if he didn't take the job, how was he going to pay what he owed?

The Town Hall clock struck one o'clock. Barry was well late. With a bit of luck the people at the hostel would let him off. First offence and all that. But supposing he didn't go back to the hostel? What if he jumped ship and just disappeared? Would anyone care? There would be nothing to show he had ever been there except a bag of dirty clothes in the hostel.

Barry realized he was walking down the street where his nan used to live. Her house was at the far end. It looked like someone had already replaced the windows with PVC ones. The front wall had been knocked down and the tiny front garden paved over. There was a taxi parked there now. Upstairs in one of the windows was a large Man U badge. It used to be Barry's bedroom. There was a light on behind the curtains in the front room, all orange and warm. Barry shivered.

Somewhere overhead a police helicopter was growling, its red lights blinking like evil eyes.

Barry stuck two fingers up. The rain was coming down more heavily now.

By the trunk road he passed a couple of girls shivering in a shop doorway. He felt sorry for them. How terrible to have to earn money like that.

'Are you OK, mate?'

'Yeah, just a bit knackered, that's all.'

'You look it. Fancy a lie down?'

Barry grinned and shook his head. 'Thanks, but – I've got to get back.' He hesitated. 'I wouldn't mind joining you under there for a minute, though.'

'Costs double for both of us!' one of the girls laughed. 'Hope you can afford it.'

He squeezed in beside them. She pulled out a pack of cigarettes. 'Want one? They're menthol.'

Barry pulled a face. 'No thanks.'

He started to roll one of his own. Then the sweet minty menthol smell hit him. Suddenly he was three or four again, sitting on the sink, watching his mum doing her nails at the kitchen table. Her mascara had run where she had been laughing. Or had she been crying? His dad was combing his hair in the mirror, all dressed up ready to go out. Upstairs he could hear Nan bathing Abi. After his mum and dad had gone out, she would let him and Abi watch television by the fire in their pyjamas. If they were good, she would open a tin of home-made treacle toffee . . .

Barry welled up with feelings of overwhelming loss. He felt sad for his mum and for his dad. For his nan. For Abi. For the happy little boy he had once been. For the childhood he and Abi had never really had. Why did his mum have to disappear like that? Didn't she love them enough? Was it their fault? He hoped she had found happiness somewhere else. But he doubted it. Some people inherited money from their parents. She had left him the only thing she had a lot of – bad luck.

Some people never had a chance. They never got to live the life they wanted. Was he one of those? Always unlucky? Would he always be outside in the rain, watching other people through a window? Wishing he was inside by the fire? All Barry wanted was to be ordinary, to be normal. He didn't want a fast car or a big house. Just a small place where he and Abi could live together. Was it so much to ask?

What do you think?

What do you think Barry should do about Abi and Little Chris?

Why do you think Barry sticks two fingers up at the police helicopter?

Why do you think Barry felt sorry for the girls standing in the shop doorway?

How responsible is Barry for what happens to him?

19

Tomorrow

———•◆•———

'Are you sure you're all right?' one of the girls said. 'You don't look it.' She put her hand on Barry's arm. He didn't trust himself to say anything. He knew that if he tried to speak he would start crying. He pushed her away and set off into the rain.

He pulled his collar tight. At least it never rained in prison. He thought about his warm bed on the 2s. Tomorrow was Sunday. Gym in the morning. A game of football on the radio in the afternoon. Chips for tea.

He thought about Gaz, Mo, Taj and all the lads who were still inside. If they had got out yesterday, would they be coping any better? What would Gaz do in his shoes? Not for the first time, Barry realized how much he was missing him.

Part of him was already beginning to wish he was back inside. Life in the nick ran along certain predictable tracks. You knew where you were. Cons on one side, screws on the other. Black and white. It was a stupid system, but at least it was a system. Of course there were plenty of idiots on both sides. But he had met some of the best lads in prison.

On the other hand, no matter how hard things were, he knew that Gaz and the others would swap places with him in a heartbeat. He owed it to them not to go back. He somehow felt he had to stay out for their sake. The system loved to see you walk back in through the gates. It thrived on failure. Of course governments liked talking about rehabilitation. But no one took the idea seriously. What would happen if no one ever went back? What if all the prisons were empty?

He looked up at the night sky. The rain was starting to ease off. The clouds shifted, luminous against the moon, showing the patient stars behind. By the time he reached the gates of the hostel it had stopped raining. The night air was warm.

He took a deep breath as he walked through the hostel gates. He knew he was going to get a bollocking for being late. But on Monday morning he had a meeting with his probation officer. Then he was going to the Job Centre. Later he might go round to Lisa's house.

But first thing tomorrow morning he was going to find a laundrette for that bag of dirty washing.

What do you think?

Why do you think Barry is homesick for prison?

What do you think would happen if there were no prisons?

What advice would you give Barry?